# Arnold the Angel

## Arnold Becomes Winnie's Guardian

ST JOSEPH'S CATHOLIC PRIMARY SCHOOL
Dorset Road
Christchurch
Dorset
BH23 3DA
Tel: **01202 485976**

# Arnold the Angel

## Arnold Becomes Winnie's Guardian

### Freda Bonard

Copyright © Freda Bonard 2019

Produced in association with

The right of Freda Bonard to be identified as the
Author of this Work has been asserted by her in accordance
with the Copyright, Designs and Patents Act 1988.

All rights reserved. No part of this publication may be reproduced,
stored in a retrieval system, or transmitted, in any form or by any means,
electronic, mechanical, photocopying, recording or otherwise,
without the prior permission of Words by Design.

ISBN: 978-1-909075-84-9

Typeset in Sabon
Printed and bound by CPI Group (UK) Ltd, Croydon, CR0 4YY

# Contents

1. Arnold, and the New Baby     1
2. Winnie's War     27
3. Winnie and the Crushed Hut     47
4. Winnie, Freddie and Robin     65
5. Winnie's Strange Visitors     83
6. St. Thomas and the Currant Buns     98
7. Winnie Goes Home     111

By the Same Author:

Arnold the Angel: The Story Begins
Arnold the Angel Becomes an Apprentice

# Acknowledgements

This book is dedicated to Norman and Barbara from the Village under the Downs.

Writing this book has been quite an emotional journey. I hadn't realised how much I had missed the village, but of course the wonderful patch of Earth where I grew up will always be so very special.

It was there that I experienced a way of life that has long since faded into history. Who among readers, for instance, has ever seen a brick copper? When I was a small child, nothing much had changed from my mother's young days.

The village is now a very different place, but it will always hold a dear place in my heart, together with all the people I remember so fondly.

I owe a great debt of thanks to my editor, Chris Lightfoot. She has guided me through again with enormous patience and I am most grateful.

I would also like to mention my friends who like to listen to my stories. They encourage me greatly.

And, as always, thank you to Michael.

# Chapter 1

# Arnold and the New Baby

Hello, my friends, as you know, my name is Arnold and I am an angel. We have shared many things together, haven't we? As we speak, I am still in a state of shock and wonder having seen Father God in all His glory in Heaven.

I have also had the privilege of being taught by the Holy Spirit. He taught a group of us young angels about God's messengers who helped people during the time before Jesus was born. Of course we didn't know who He was at first and it was only when we saw Him in glory with Our Father and Jesus that we realised. He had also shown us some of the astonishing things which Father God had created in Heaven. We were now much wiser and ready for our next job in service to Father God.

From Father God's beautiful room, I went directly to the Guardian Angel Assignment Office to find out what God had in mind for me. There I met Claude, a huge old angel who had seen it all. His office was stacked with files.

"Hello, young Arnold," he said. "I hear Our Father has a job for you. Come this way, and I will tell you about it."

I went to stand by Claude's desk. "Here we are", he said, pulling out one of his files from a tottering heap. "God told me to show you this."

Claude showed me what looked like a family tree. "Now then. This is the family you will join. As country people, they have always worked on the land and they are used to working hard for a living, but they are good people who love God and want to bring their children up in the right way. God wants you to be Guardian Angel for a little girl who is just about to be born. He knows that she is going to have a hard life and she needs an Angel to love her and take special care of her. Father God thinks you are just the Angel for the job."

"Now, come with me." Claude took me to a huge window at the back of his office.

*Harvest time*

"Look down there," he said. From this high place, I could see a house with a sparkling marker over it and several other Guardian Angels fluttering round nervously. "There you are, my boy!" he boomed, "welcome to your new post! Don't forget to report to Father God every so often. You know He loves to hear how His children are getting on." With that he opened his office door and I found myself outside the house with the marker.

I was sent to look after Winnie.

I was to be her Guardian Angel and this time, I didn't need any help.

Winnie lived with her family in a country village which nestled at the foot of rolling hills, known as the Downs. It was a pretty place. In spring the air smelled of the blossom, pink and white, which frothed on all the fruit trees which surrounded the village. The farmers grew apples, pears and cherries. They were very proud of the fact that their apples were among the best in the country.

The other special activity in the village was the training of race horses. There were several stables and early every morning a string of horses, each with a stable lad, could be seen walking quietly up the hill out of the village to their 'gallops' at the top of the Downs.

The village had a school and a church. There was a shop and a public house and as the villagers also had a parish hall, they thought themselves very fortunate. No one had a car and so if they wanted to get out of the village they either walked, rode their bicycles or got the bus.

Winnie was born at home. This was at a time when there was no running water in the house. The water had to be brought in from the pump which was shared by twelve houses. There was no electricity either. The house was lit by beautiful oil lamps or candles. If you wanted a bath, you had to bring in the tin bath which was hung up on the wall outside and boil water in the brick copper in the kitchen. Incidentally, the only toilet in the house was outside too. You had to go out of the back door and go round the corner to an outside door. There, in all its glory was a dry toilet. It was home to every type of spider you could think of and, as there was no light either, a trip to the loo in the night could be a very scary experience.

It only took me a few minutes to find out how the family lived. It was very important for me to understand as I would be with Winnie and her family for many years. I had a good look round the house and discovered how difficult life could be for people living in the country at that time. The other Guardian Angels caring for the family were called Tom, Dick and Harry. We became great friends and they were very helpful.

I found out that cooking was done on a range which was heated by a fire on one side and had an oven on the other. Water could be heated on the top.

Wash day was heavy work. A fire was lit under the copper in the kitchen and the washing was put in the water to boil. The only problem was that if the water boiled over, there was no way to stop it and you just had to get out of the way while boiling water flooded the floor. Winnie's mother had a vast mangle – a device with rollers on it that squeezed the water out of the clothes when you turned the handle. That was very hard work too and you had to be very careful that you didn't squeeze your fingers.

The little girl was born into a time when everyone made do with what they had. For instance, there were several rugs in their home which had been made by threading rags into a sack. Winnie's favourite was the one coloured black and red made out of a pair of her father's old trousers and an old red flannel night shirt.

Bed-side tables were made of wooden orange boxes, which were placed on their ends so that there was a shelf in the middle. These were then covered with wall paper and fitted with material from one of Winnie's mother's old summer dresses to make a curtain on the front.

There was no heating upstairs, so the winter nights were very cold. Heavy dressing gowns were added to the blankets on the beds to keep everyone warm. Everyone had a stone hot water bottle which was filled with boiling water and wrapped in an old clean jumper or towel. This was very comforting in the severe cold of the winters in the deep countryside.

In the living room a washing line made of string was festooned with ironed clothes to 'air' them. Of course there was no other way of doing it.

Winnie's father was a blacksmith. He had a forge and workshop at the other end of the village. He worked long hours for not much money but he was expert at making horse shoes and mending farm machinery. Winnie's mother had been housemaid to the old priest. She then became one of the maids to the aristocratic family who lived in the Big House. When she got married she earned a little money by cleaning for some of the more well-off people in the village.

They had an older son called Patrick. He was thrilled to know that he would soon have a baby brother or sister. All their lives Winnie and Patrick loved each other very much.

On the day that Winnie was born, a lady from the next village came to help with the birth. This was also in the times when there were no district nurses and so there was usually a woman who lived nearby who delivered babies and helped out when people died. In this case the lady's name was Sarah and she just happened to be Winnie's aunt. She was well trusted in the

*Winnie, aged 13*

area as she could always be relied upon to come when needed most.

I arrived at Winnie's home just as she was born. I joined with all the other Guardian Angels in the house in celebrating the new arrival.

Winnie's father and brother were pacing anxiously downstairs as Sarah placed the baby gently in a drawer she had taken out of the dressing table and lined with soft towels.

I went into the bedroom and gazed down at my new charge. I realised, even then, that Winnie would be a strong and determined character, as she looked me straight in the eye. Did I ever tell you that babies can see their Guardian Angels when they are first born? Winnie seemed to be sizing me up to see if I was equal to the task.

You have probably gathered that Winnie was born into quite a poor family. Her mother could not afford a cot for her new baby so the drawer worked just as well. It was the drawer which she had used for her son Patrick. Friends and neighbours had given some hand-me-down clothes and one or two toys, but that was all they had.

Still, they were a happy little family and my job as a Guardian Angel was quite easy. That all changed when Winnie learned to walk. As soon as she was mobile she was determined to have adventures, like the day she let the chickens out. Winnie had always been told not to play with the chickens. Her father happened to look out of the window to see all his chickens happily scratching in his newly prepared seed bed. He ran outside, angrily asking Winnie why she had let them out. She looked up at him defiantly and said, "I didn't let them out. I just opened the door and they walked out!"

What could you say to that?

I had been going to report to Father God every month or so. He had been so interested in everything I had to tell Him and encouraged me to bring him all the news I could about my little charge, Winnie.

I was also trying to work out how to communicate with the little girl. Sometimes I gave her gentle dreams to tell her how much I loved her. Other times I was able to whisper softly in her ear to help her make decisions or keep her from getting lost.

On one occasion she had gone for a walk with an older friend and a huge sheep charged at her and pinned her against a fence. I may have told you that animals can see angels, so the sheep was very surprised to see an angry angel with outspread wings, telling him firmly to leave Winnie alone.

Winnie was soon going about the village by herself. In those days children were quite safe to wander in a place where everyone knew them.

Winnie loved going to see the cobbler in the village. He was a man who was quite disabled and had been taught to mend shoes so that he could make a living for himself. She used to sit in his workshop chattering happily to him and watching as he expertly cut leather and nailed it to the soles of men's shoes, or fitted rubber heels to women's shoes. She liked the smell of the glue he used. He had a little stumpy stick which he used to get a glob of glue onto the shoe and spread it over the sole. Winnie was fascinated by the way the cobbler held a row of the little nails he used to fix the leather to the shoes in his mouth. She thought it made him look like a big fish.

Next to the cobbler's garden was a field which belonged to the public house. On one of her visits she saw three boys beating up another boy in the field. She knew this boy and knew he would have difficulty defending himself. Besides, she didn't like bullying, and she was also fearless. So she climbed over the fence and waded in with all her strength. The three bullies were so surprised, they ran off. I was surprised too. She caught me completely off guard. From then on I learned that Winnie could be unpredictable, particularly when she thought people were being treated unfairly.

Generally, Winnie liked school. The school house was very basic. It had just one big room which was divided into two classrooms by a long green curtain. There was a huge coke boiler in the middle of the room which was their only source of heat. This was fine except when something went wrong and both classes were filled with poisonous fumes. These were the days on which everyone went for a nature walk. Close to the school there was a vast wood, known as the 'Plantation'. Everyone in the village enjoyed walking there, especially when the wild daffodils were out.

I might just make an aside here. The children in the village knew where to find the best wild flowers. The other good place was the cemetery where thousands of snowdrops grew every year. It didn't occur to them that perhaps they shouldn't pick them – it was just nice to take something home for their mothers after one of their walks.

In those days there were always many wild flowers to see. Poppies, cornflowers, dog roses and smaller flowers that you really had to search for, like the shy little violets that you could usually find by their scent. The children loved to make daisy chains and could be seen sitting on the grass to see who could make the longest.

With a bottle of water and a jam sandwich, the children could be out all day long and the summer days never seemed to end.

Winnie was an intelligent little girl. The children learned to write using slates and chalk. To learn their sums, they were given flat tobacco tins filled with sea shells. You could add up and take away, using the shells to count. There were always twenty shells in a tin and at the end of the lesson twenty shells had to be counted back in. Painting was one of the children's favourites. They were given sheets of newspaper to paint on. There were no art lessons as such, the children were just told what to paint. Years later, Winnie could recall the smell of the poster paints. It brought back many happy memories of her days at the village school.

On wet days, out would come the jigsaws and building bricks. The children liked this best of all.

On the down side, the teacher was very strict. On Monday mornings, the children were asked if they had been to church. If they had not they were punished. This always seemed unfair to Winnie, as some of the children lived a long way from church and couldn't get there by themselves.

They had to learn the catechism by heart. This was a book of rules of the Church and how children were taught about God. Winnie didn't think much of this either, as there was lots of learning, but not much explanation. Every week the old priest would come in to the school and test the children on their catechism. At the end of the term there was always a little prize for the child who had answered the most questions right. Needless to say, Winnie never won.

Winnie had a friend called Daphne. They played very happily together. One of their favourite things was setting each other's hair with a fish paste pot full of water and an old comb.

At Christmas, because times were hard, children could only expect one or two presents. This might include a stocking with nuts and an orange. Winnie was delighted one Christmas when she was given a doll's bed made out of a wooden fruit box. Her mother and the lady next door had dressed the box with scraps of material and made a little pillow. This was Winnie's most treasured possession.

This, though, led to one of the worst fights Winnie and her brother Patrick ever had. Winnie came home from school one day to find her dolls hanging by their necks out of the bedroom window. She soon showed Patrick what she thought of him even though she was punished for kicking him in the shin.

I enjoyed Winnie's company immensely. She was tough and fearless and you knew exactly where you were with her. Father God loved to hear about her latest adventures and sent her special blessings which I took to her with pride.

Things began to change for Winnie as she grew older. It may have been because there were rumours of war and her mother was anxious about her son joining the navy, but something had hardened in her mother's attitude towards her.

Winnie found herself being treated almost like a housemaid. It was her job to scrub the concrete kitchen floor every Saturday morning and cycle four miles to the nearest town to do the weekly shopping. This was difficult as it was a very hilly route and balancing heavy bags on her handlebars was not easy.

As her Guardian Angel, I travelled alongside Winnie as she rode to protect her from passing traffic. I also tried to send her my love, to keep her spirits up and to let her know she was not alone.

Winnie also had to cycle to secondary school which was over six miles away. Yes, life was becoming tough.

Father God was sad to hear that Winnie was having a hard time and He asked me to whisper in her ear to say some extra prayers to Jesus. As He said, Jesus knew how difficult life could be on Earth and would help to give her courage.

*Winnie's mother and father*

The dreaded war had started and all the young men were going off to fight.

Not only that, there had been some terrible bombing in most of the big cities. This meant that thousands of children had to be sent away to the country to be kept safe. These children were called evacuees and two little boys were sent to live with Winnie's family. They were called Arthur and Wally and they came to love the village and all the people in it.

They got on very well with Winnie. She would take them out for walks and rides on their bikes. She played board games with them and helped them write letters home. They were very fond of her and thought she was great fun.

One day, however, Winnie came home to find that there were two more people in their already crowded house. A woman called Mrs. Ramsay and her daughter had been evacuated after they had been bombed out. This kind of thing was only to be expected considering how dangerous life in cities could be, but what upset Winnie was the fact that her mother had given Mrs. Ramsay's daughter Winnie's new nightdress. Now Winnie would not have minded if she had been able to give the nightdress herself. What upset her most was the fact that her mother did not seem to understand that doing something like this might be hurtful.

But instead of feeling too sorry for herself, she threw herself into village life, such as it was.

She loved to dance. There were regular dances in the village hall and all the girls dressed up in their prettiest frocks and looked forward to an enjoyable evening out. One of Winnie's friends was called Peggy. They always walked to the dances together, chatting and laughing. This was another time when I kept a close eye on Winnie – I wanted to keep her safe, for a very good reason.

Winnie was in love! She was about sixteen and had left school. She had a job of her own on the local fruit farm and she had a little money to spend for the first time in her life.

Winnie's boyfriend Bertie came from the next village and would ride over on his bike to see her. She met him at one of the village dances and, although he had two left feet, Winnie liked him straight away. He was kind and considerate and a few years older. Winnie's father also liked him at once, although it took a bit of time for her mother to come round.

Bertie had signed up to join the army. He was due to go abroad soon. Winnie had just turned seventeen and they asked her parents if they could get married before he went. To Winnie's great joy and delight, they said yes.

Well, as everyone said, "There's a War on!"

Rationing had been in force for some time and getting food together for a reception was not going to be easy.

Not only that, but what about the wedding dress?

This is where I came in. I went round the village talking to all the other Guardian Angels and explaining to them what I wanted. They in turn whispered inspiration in their peoples' ears and, before long, folk came with coupons for flour and fat to make cakes and for sugar and cheese – in fact anything that was on ration that they could think of. This was most generous as rationing was very tight and they would have to go without themselves.

But what about the wedding dress? Miraculously one day a bolt of parachute silk turned up. In the war it didn't do to enquire too closely where things had come from, so Winnie didn't. Parachute silk made many a First Communion or Confirmation dress. What could you do when things were in such a state in the country?

# Chapter 2

# Winnie's War

This was the time I got to know Bertie's Guardian Angel. He was called Horace and he looked after Bertie very well. I like to think that we worked well together and we were very excited to go to Father God together to tell him about the forthcoming wedding.

The young couple were getting married in the little village church. It was where Winnie's parents were married and where she and her brother were baptised.

The great day dawned.

As the service started Horace and I stood proudly behind our charges and poured out all the love that God had sent and all of our own.

Friends and family had made the sometimes difficult journey to help celebrate their happy day. The little church looked lovely. Neighbours and friends had raided their own gardens for summer flowers and had made beautiful arrangements for the altar.

Winnie's brother was away at sea, so couldn't be there, but his wife came and she was expecting their first child. That was such special news.

After the service everyone walked about half-a-mile to the village hall. There, laid out on a long table, was a wartime feast.

But what of the wedding cake?

Sugar was rationed as I told you, so there was no icing. But there was a beautiful white cake, with a ribbon round it and everything – how had they done it? On closer inspection, it could be seen that the cake was encased in a white cardboard shell. Underneath was a chocolate cake which everyone enjoyed anyway.

Winnie looked beautiful in her silk dress and Bertie was married in his uniform and sported a carnation in his button hole.

After the reception everyone went outside and photographs were taken. In those days,

*Winnie and Bertie are married*

photos were always in black and white and taken by one of the family with a little Box Brownie camera. All her life, Winnie treasured those photos, keeping them safe in an old biscuit tin.

Their honeymoon consisted of a long weekend in a nearby big town where they stayed with Bertie's aunt and uncle. Only a few days later Bertie had to return to his regiment and Winnie didn't see him again for many months. That was one of the great sorrows of war.

All during the time of the wedding, I was kept very busy. I talked to all the Guardian Angels, especially the ones of people who had to travel. Winnie's sister-in-law, for instance, lived in a town with a naval base. This was one of the towns which suffered the worst bombing in the country. Margie's angel had his work cut out to keep her safe, I can tell you.

Bertie's angel, Horace, also had a hard time of it. Bertie was in the thick of the fighting.

He was a very steady man and the young officer in charge of his unit depended on him for his experience and wisdom and his courage under fire.

Everyone in the village wanted to "do their bit" to help in the war effort. Of course, all the young men had gone away, called up to the Army, Navy or Air Force.

The older men, some of whom of course had served in the First World War, volunteered to be Home Guards. They all had their own jobs as well and every spare inch was used to grow vegetables. Winnie and her friend Peggy were drafted to a big munitions factory where cars had been made before the war. They cycled seven miles every day, did a twelve hour shift and then cycled seven miles back. This wasn't too bad on a bright summer's morning but in the winter they very nearly froze to death.

They were making spare parts for fighter planes, which involved standing in front of a huge machine and twisting knobs and pulling levers. Working conditions were not good. The factory was cold and the floor was always wet. They were supplied with wooden clogs to wear to keep their feet out of the water. There was also a very strict supervisor. You had to ask to go to the toilet and the supervisor timed you. If you took too long, your wages were docked.

Gradually Winnie began to feel ill. She had very little energy and she felt weak and breathless. This made it difficult for her to stand at her machine for all those hours and it was almost impossible for her to cycle up the hills on the way home. Winnie, being the tough and stubborn character that she was, declared that she had to keep working because of the war and she must keep doing her bit towards the war effort.

I was very concerned about her. I went to Father God and explained how poorly Winnie was. Our Father said that he had a plan and that I should keep whispering to her to go the doctor. This, of course, I did. Winnie kept going to work until one day she fainted. She was taken home in a drafty old lorry with her bike in the back and was at last seen by a doctor. He said she was suffering from anaemia, which meant her blood didn't have enough iron. After a course of tablets she began to feel better but it was thought she should not go back to the factory.

This was when Winnie and Peggy went back to work on the fruit farm. In it's own way, this was also back-breaking work but it was out in the open air and, as the farm was in the village, they didn't have that dreadful ride to the factory. There was also a chicken battery on the farm and one of the jobs of the day was to collect the eggs. There were thousands of hens in small cages in the battery and collecting the eggs took most of the morning. However, Winnie had very nimble fingers and so she was quick and efficient.

This was Father God's plan. Winnie was able to do her bit for the war effort and stay healthy and fit as well.

Winnie and her friend soon became expert at pruning the fruit trees. This was a cold job. If it had been raining, icy water would run up their sleeves as they reached up to the branches to clip off the surplus twigs to make sure the apple trees produced a good harvest the next season.

It was at this time that I discovered just how fearless Winnie was.

In a war, some men are captured and kept prisoner. This was why there was a camp nearby where German and Italian prisoners lived out the rest of their war. They were expected to work and so several prisoners were brought to the fruit farm each day.

Mostly this worked quite well because, as Winnie discovered, most of them were ordinary family men who only wanted the war to be over and to go home.

This changed when a tall, handsome man came. He was blond and had blue eyes, and he was very arrogant. They called him Fritz because he would not tell them his true name. He also declared that he would not work for the British. He had not reckoned on meeting Winifred.

She faced right up to him and, although much shorter, she looked him straight in the eye and asked who he thought he was. She said he was fortunate that he had not been killed, or kept in one of the dreadful camps run by other countries. She said, "You will work, the same as all of us!" As you might imagine, I had a stern word with Fritz's angel who in turn spoke some stern words in the young man's ear. Fritz backed down and, from then on, became a very useful member of their team.

Fritz turned out to be very fit and athletic. There was an old horse who pulled a cart along the rows of trees when the workers were pruning or picking apples. One of

Fritz's favourite tricks was to get the horse to canter along and he would vault over him again and again. This made everyone laugh and clap, but the horse was not at all impressed. After all, his usual speed was a quiet amble.

This old horse also loved strong peppermints. The only problem was they made him very windy.

There was another prisoner of war working on the farm called Heinz. He was a gentle family man, who could not do enough for the women who were also working there. He had a little tin in his pocket and could be seen collecting the little dribbles of sap which formed on the bark of the fruit trees. He said he used it as glue when he made little toys to send home to his children. If he was ever given a sweet, that would also go in the tin. He said conditions in his home country were worse than in Britain, so his children had nothing and, for all he knew, were starving.

Heinz became a family friend, and Winnie's mother invited him to Christmas dinner several years running.

Margie meanwhile had given birth to a lovely little girl. They named her Pattie after her father. She was blonde and blue eyed and, when she learned to walk, Margie made sure she came to stay in the village. Pattie loved to go to the fruit farm where everyone spoiled her. This included Heinz who could be seen helping her to ride the old cow which was the other animal resident on the farm.

During all this time, we, the Guardian Angels, were whispering peace and encouragement into our people's ears. We knew how difficult it was for everyone and we did what we could to help.

Winnie had something else to occupy her spare time. There was a big old house in the village which could be reached by going through a five-bar gate. The house had not been lived in for many years and the grounds were overgrown. But, in the area around the house were several Nissen huts which had been used for storage in the First World War. A Nissen hut is shaped like a tunnel and has quite a lot of space inside. A few of the young couples in the village had been allowed to try to make homes out of them. This included Winnie and her husband.

On one of Bertie's brief home leaves, they went to work with gusto. They cleaned the inside first. What a job that was. Bertie divided the hut using hardboard into two rooms so that they had a bedroom and a sitting-room-cum-kitchen. They were given several pieces of furniture by friends and were allowed to buy what was called utility furniture which was very plain and sturdy. In fact Winnie used a utility tallboy throughout her married life. A tallboy is a storage cupboard with drawers at the top and doors below. In later years it stood in her bedroom painted white.

Winnie's friend Peggy made some lovely curtains for the only window and she also made them a beautiful white tablecloth with their initials worked into the corners in very fine crochet.

Winnie was very proud of her cooking arrangements. She had a cooker fired by oil which worked something like her mother's range. She found she could make a very nice cake in the little oven as long as she kept a close eye on it.

Bertie was able to make a small fireplace in the sitting room and once they had got rid of the damp they were very warm and cosy.

Of course there was no electricity but they had been given a lovely old oil lamp which they carried from room to room when necessary. This worked very well too. Water could be brought in from a standpipe in the grounds and so they felt very fortunate to have a little home of their own.

However, one night, Father God sent for me. He told me some terrible news and said it would be too much of a shock for Winnie without a bit of warning. Father told me to speak to her in a dream. Of course I bowed before the Throne and hurried to do as I was asked.

That night, as Winnie lay in her bed, I showed her two pictures. The first was of her brother Patrick. In the picture he was ill in a hospital bed. In the dream Winnie wiped Patrick's face but, as he turned his head towards her, his face turned into Bertie's.

Winnie woke up, shaking with fear and for many days could not get the images out of her mind. This was just as well because within a month the dreadful news of her brother's death was brought to the family by telegram. He was being brought home on a hospital ship because he had a fever. While at sea, the ship was torpedoed and sank losing thousands of men.

*Patrick and his American friend*

This was the worst news that any family could hear. Patrick's father never really recovered from the shock. As I mentioned before, Winnie was very close to her brother and the loss of Patrick clouded her life for the rest of her days.

As if this was not bad enough, they got the news that Bertie had been wounded. He was brought to a hospital about twelve miles from the village so Winnie could visit him. He had a severe injury to his left arm and he was in plaster for months. The only good thing was that he did not have to go back into the army.

Horace and I worked hard during this difficult time. We guarded the couple during the day and kept watch at night, praying to our Father in Heaven to give them some comfort.

Father God had been greatly saddened by the terrible war going on all over His beautiful world. On one of my visits I got up the courage to ask Him why He allowed such a dreadful thing to happen. He sighed and said that He loved His people so much that he had given them free will. This meant that they could choose whether to do good or go down a bad path. God also said that because of this, He had to send His only Son, Jesus, to take on all the sins ever committed in the world and also the punishment that should have been given to His people. Horace and I were filled with greater love than ever for this wonderful Creator God. It was almost too much to take in. We knelt on the floor of God's beautiful room and worshipped at our Father's feet.

When Bertie got home, it was very difficult for him to settle back into village life. Night after night he would sit up in bed shouting and screaming at his nightmares. He would never say what he had seen in the war, but he was haunted by dreadful memories for a long time.

Gradually, things began to calm down. Winnie and Bertie enjoyed living in their little hut and everything was getting to a good place, until the night of the storm.

# Chapter 3

# Winnie and the Crushed Hut

There was a film that Bertie wanted to see. The young couple had planned to go one Saturday evening. They got the bus and chatted all the way to town, looking forward to a night out together.

As they travelled, Bertie noticed that the wind was getting up. He saw that the tree tops were thrashing about and the clouds were racing across the moon. Still they didn't let the weather worry them. They had lived through gales before, after all.

When they got off the bus, a sudden gust of wind took Winnie's hat and blew it over the road. Bertie, ever the gentleman, retrieved it, and they went laughing into the cinema. They enjoyed the film very much and talked about it all the way home.

They walked home from the bus stop, still chattering happily when what a sad sight met their eyes!.

A huge tree had been blown down and crushed their little home. Winnie burst into tears. Their first home together had been destroyed. All their hard work had been for nothing. They stood, side-by-side, looking sadly at the mess. There was nothing they could do about it in the dark and the wind. The only thing to be done was to go to Winnie's parents for the night and see what the morning would bring.

The next day proved to be worse than even they had thought. The only things they could salvage were a mantel clock, Winnie's wedding photos and the utility tallboy. They managed to rescue a few of their clothes, but that was all.

Pattie was staying with her grandmother for a few days and she did what she could to cheer the young couple up. She went with them when they were trying to salvage some of their belongings and tried to help them move back to the other house.

There was nothing else for it. They had to move back in to Winnie's childhood home and they never had the chance to move out to a home of their own for many years. During this time Winnie was very sad for quite a while. It was the first time that she suffered from depression. Her parents did what they could to make them comfortable, however. There was a little room at the front of the house which her parents used as their sitting room so that Winnie and Bertie could have some privacy in the main living room.

As Winnie's Guardian Angel I felt sorry for her. I was also aware that there was a bad angel lurking around trying to make Winnie feel worse. I stood guard over her at night to make sure this bad one could not interfere with her dreams and I brought in several of my Heavenly friends to cluster round her all the time she felt bad. Eventually we managed to get rid of it and after a while Winnie began to feel better and was able to get on with life again.

Winnie and her mother had never had an easy relationship. The atmosphere was always edgy between them. When the two ladies were arguing, Bertie would wander down the garden with his hands in his pockets whistling to himself. He could very often be found there messing about in his shed. He was, however, very fond of his father-in-law. They worked in the garden together and Bertie helped wherever he could.

We have got a bit in front of ourselves. As I told you, Bertie's arm was in plaster for many months. One Sunday afternoon, Bertie could not be found. Winnie was quite worried about him, because he still was not up to full health after his injury. She got on her bike, and went round the village calling at their friends' houses, asking if anyone had seen him. No one had.

Suddenly, she heard faint cheering. It was coming from the direction of the recreation ground, at the other end of the village. Winnie had an inspiration. She rode as quickly as she could towards the cheering.

There was a football match taking place. Was Bertie watching? Indeed he was not. There he was, arm in plaster, playing in the match and having a wonderful time! As he said later, they were a man down and he couldn't let the team down, could he?

Another time, there was a dance in the village hall. Winnie loved to dance as I may have mentioned. She and Bertie and their friend Peggy arrived at the village hall to find that a busload of American servicemen had come. Now this could be tricky. For one thing, the Americans were paid a great deal more than their British counterparts. This caused jealousy and friction among the younger men in the village, especially the stable lads.

It wasn't long before a fight broke out. Bertie had spent a while serving in the military police and so he thought he ought to do something to break it up. Arm still in plaster, he made his way to the middle of the fight. He was very strong and thought he could separate the young men with one hand. He would have, too, but for the fact that Winnie and Peggy pulled him away and sat on him.

All the Guardian Angels did what they could to calm things down. Bertie's angel, Horace, was quite used to Bertie trying to do the right thing. He didn't seem to understand that there were limitations. Horace whispered calmness and peace in Bertie's ear and gradually all returned to an enjoyable night out for everyone.

I was beginning to understand what an extraordinary person Winnie was. Not always easy to get on with, she had a very quick temper which could flare up out of nowhere. However, she had a wicked sense of humour and a razor sharp wit. This didn't stop her from being one of the kindest people you would ever meet. She had an amazing talent for caring for people who were poorly.

This didn't stretch to someone who she didn't think were helping themselves. When

Bertie's plaster was taken off, he had very little movement in his left hand. He really thought that his working life was over and that he had done his bit. Again, he hadn't reckoned with his young wife. She came home one day to find Bertie sitting in the living room reading the paper.

She had just done a heavy day's work on the fruit farm and she was tired. Bertie barely looked up when she came in and of course Winnie's temper flared.

The next day when she came home, she told him in no uncertain terms that she had given up her job and what was he going to do about it?

Of course Bertie was still in no fit state to do a full day's work, so this was one of the few times in his life that he really lost his temper. Within a few days, he acquired some old railway sleepers and started to build a shed at the bottom of the garden. He was able to get rid of all his frustrations but, as you can imagine, building a shed with one hand is a very difficult thing.

He found that he had to use the fingers of his left hand to hold the nails. He could be heard swearing and howling with pain as he hit his fingers with the hammer, but gradually, the shed was built.

This was the beginning of a lifetime of hard work. When Bertie was fit, he worked on a farm for a long time and then he worked at the local small railway station, where he won a prize for the best kept station waiting room. He was very proud of that, as you can imagine. Winnie, meanwhile, hadn't really given up her job.

She worked on the fruit farm for many years, despite the fact that she had a very bad back. She wore corsets with stiff steels in the back and this helped her with all the heavy lifting she had to do as part of her job. She could swing a bushel of apples, which weighed forty pounds, from the ground up onto a lorry. She said it was all a knack, but I'm sure most people couldn't do it.

One of Bertie's greatest regrets was that he had been offered an apprenticeship in one of the big estate gardens when he was young. However, his mother would not let him go, This would have changed his life for the better, but throughout his life the garden was his greatest love.

Bertie's vegetables were legendary in the village. He entered the village shows, and usually came away with several prizes. He planted everything in straight lines, even daffodils, and his garden was always beautifully kept.

He used to love to take little Pattie for walks. He helped her find the violets which she loved to take home for her grandmother, or sometimes, Winnie. He showed her the animals grazing in the fields and held her up so she could stroke their noses.

One of their favourite walks on a Sunday afternoon was to the next village to see Aunt Sarah, Uncle Lawrence and Aunt Emily.

Sarah was Winnie's father's sister and Emily was his twin. You may remember that Sarah was the lady who helped deliver babies and helped out when people died. Winnie and Bertie loved them all dearly.

Emily was born 'delicate'. She had a slightly twisted neck and could not walk very well. This meant that she could not earn her own living or get married, so Sarah and Lawrence kept her with them. She could, however, do the most marvellous knitting and crochet work, so she was able to make a little money by knitting garments to order.

She would sit by the fire, smiling in a gentle way, and watch everything that happened. She was also very deaf. She had a hearing aid which had an enormous battery pack that was as big as a handbag.

*Emily, Lawrence, Sarah and Skinny the cat*

Poor Emily's health was not improved by the fact that she had a series of severe strokes. This meant that she was totally dependent on Sarah and Lawrence. Sarah had given her life to looking after everyone in the village and she was tired out. However, this didn't stop her from caring for Emily. It did mean though, that looking after her disabled sister was almost too much for her.

So, what does Winnie do? After a heavy day's work she got on her bike and cycled to the next village to help put Emily to bed. There was no other help to be had and, although it was exhausting, Winnie was glad to do it. Winnie did this for several years and, of course, travelling on dark winter nights produced several adventures.

Some nights, Winnie would choose to walk along a main road which ran along the top of the village. She would take their old dog for company but the trouble was, the dog was scared of the dark. Every time he heard a rustle in the hedge, he would shrink into

Winnie's legs and refuse to move until she assured him that there was nothing to be frightened of.

I have to confess that I was responsible for scaring poor Winnie half to death. One dark moonless night Winnie was cycling home after putting Emily to bed and, as she often did, was singing to herself. I became aware that there was someone on the narrow path several yards in front of her.

This was one of the village men taking his dogs for a walk before bed. I went and asked the dogs to get off the path so that Winnie could get past safely. They obligingly pulled their master into the hedge. Winnie, meanwhile, was cycling merrily along, singing her song. As she drew alongside, all she could hear was gruff whispering and snuffling coming from low to the ground. She had no idea what was going on and she was scared witless. She started to scream and was still screaming ten minutes later when she reached home.

Bertie at once got on his bike and rode as fast as he could to the narrow path to see what had happened. He met the man with his two big dogs who explained that suddenly the animals had pulled him into the hedge and he was trying to keep them quiet so that he wouldn't frighten Winnie on her way past. I was so sorry. From then on I decided I would let things take their course unless Winnie was in danger.

Bertie's parents lived in the same village as Sarah and Lawrence. Sometimes the young couple would visit them for tea. Bertie had never been close to his own family. This was evident when he discovered that his mother had sold all of his clothes while he was away in the army.

Still, he was sorry that his step-father was very ill and he did what he could to help.

One night at about three o'clock in the morning there was a loud banging on the front door. Bertie was on the night shift at the railway station so was not at home. Winnie nervously came down the stairs and asked who was there.

It turned out to be Percy, Bertie's half-brother. He had ridden through deep snow to ask Winnie to come as their father had taken a turn for the worse. Winnie immediately got dressed and put on her heavy coat and followed Percy back to the next village. I kept as close to Winnie as I could. I even asked my Heavenly friends to lend a hand as I was sure that Winnie could use all the help she could get.

When Winnie and Percy reached the house they found Bertie's mother, his half-sister and his other half-brother sitting by the fire drinking tea.

Winnie asked where her father-in-law was. "Upstairs," was the reply. They didn't even offer her a cup of tea, obviously expecting Winnie to take charge of the situation.

Winnie went upstairs and into the bedroom. All of us angels went in with her. As she feared, her father-in-law had died. His angel sadly told us that he had carried his soul to Heaven some while before.

This could have been a very scary situation for Winnie. After all, she was all by herself in the middle of the night with a dead body to deal with. However, we the angels clustered around the old man's bed and softly sang songs of Heaven and Our Father's love. Of course Winnie couldn't hear us but she felt comforted and braver.

Winnie got her father-in-law's body ready for his funeral then rode back through the deep snow and howling blizzard. She reached home just after six in the morning. She made herself a hot drink and tried to thaw herself out by the fire. Then at eight o'clock she was back at work on the farm.

I couldn't have been more proud of my tough and caring Winnie. I went directly to

Father God and told Him the whole story. Father God at once sent Winnie a special blessing and told me a lovely secret.

# Chapter 4

# Winnie, Freddie and Robin

Winnie was going to have a baby.

Horace and I were beside ourselves with joy.

For the next nine months we, the Guardian Angels, cared for our charges even more carefully. Bertie was pleased but nervous. He took his responsibilities as a new father very seriously and he wanted to do everything he could to make sure all was ready for the new arrival.

Winnie's father also wanted to do what he could. He paid for an electric light to be fitted on the stairs so that Winnie would be safe carrying the baby up and down.

Winnie was not terribly well during her pregnancy. As you may imagine, she just carried on with her work as normal. As the time for the baby to be born drew nearer, the doctor thought it would be safer for Winnie to have the baby in hospital.

She was taken to the hospital in the big town. She was there for a whole week before the baby was born, and during that time, Winnie became ill and exhausted. It took a long time for the baby to be born and here I must tell you about the proudest moment I ever had.

The baby was born with a cleft lip and palate. This is a deformity of the nose and upper lip and the roof of the mouth. This was not really surprising, as Bertie had been born with the same thing. Didn't I tell you about this before? No? Well, it didn't seem important, as, with or without his deformity, Bertie was handsome and Winnie's favourite description of him was 'wholesome'.

There was a young woman on the ward whose baby had been born with the same condition. This lady was finding it very hard to accept. She made it known that she didn't want the baby and asked the nurses to take it away. Winnie heard about this, and taking her own baby to see her, kindly encouraged her and helped her to see that there was hope. With Winnie's advice and love, the young lady learned to love her baby and joyfully took her home.

At this point, Father God sent for me again. He said that as I was becoming an experienced Guardian Angel, He was going to give me some supervisory duties. He asked me to go and see Claude in the Guardian Angel Assignment Office as soon as I could so as I could to be introduced to my new apprentice.

I flew there as fast as I could, feeling nervous but excited.

There was Claude, surrounded as ever by his heaps of files. There also was a tiny angel, shivering with fright. Claude clapped me on the back and said how glad he was to see me again. "This here is young Robin," he said. "Father God told me that there is a new baby in your household and has assigned Robin to be its Guardian. As you can see, Robin is scared to death and he will need a great deal of support. Do you think you can help him?"

Robin and I looked at each other. He was so nervous he could barely stand up. I suddenly realised he was scared of me.

I smiled in what I hoped was an encouraging way and knelt on the floor beside him. "Hello, Robin," I said. "Will you let me help you to look after the new baby?"

Robin gazed at me with enormous eyes. He stuttered something which I couldn't make out. "Come on, young angel," boomed Claude. "What's the matter with you?"

"The honour is just too much, Sir," Robin replied. "After all, this is the great Arnold who looked after Jesus. Father God has given me such a blessing and I can't believe He has been so good to me. I'm not sure I can live up to what is expected of me."

I was speechless! Here was this young angel almost paralysed with hero worship. I wanted to laugh out loud, but I realised this would hurt his feelings, so I gently asked him to sit down with me so that we could talk. Claude took us to a bench just outside his office, from where we had a magnificent view of the whole world.

"Look at this," I said to him. "This is what our Father God has made. To Him be the glory! Yes, I was given the great privilege of being Guardian Angel to Jesus, but I started as you are. There is an Angel called Jabez who helped me every step of the way, showing me how to do things properly. I'm sure I would have made a terrible mess of things without his help and guidance. I'm just an ordinary angel. I had to do an apprenticeship after I came back to Heaven and I have great help even now from the other angels in the family. I am caring for a lady called Winnie and she has just had her baby. This is a very precious baby and Father God has put His trust in you to care for it. You will not be alone. I will help you as much as I can. However, don't forget that the only Person who deserves our worship and thanks is Father God Himself. You know that really, don't you? You and I are going to be great friends and we will start by introducing you to the other angels in the house. Are you ready?"

Robin had visibly relaxed. He heaved a great sigh, and stood up. "Yes, Arnold, I'm ready," he said and, hand in hand, we flew to the house just as Winnie arrived with her new baby.

Robin went to the pram and shyly looked in. As soon as he saw the baby, he fell in love with her.

Yes, Winnie had given birth to a baby girl. They called her Freddie and they couldn't have been happier.

Horace was standing proudly by, and so were Dick and Harry. Tom, Patrick's angel also came to see the new baby. Freddie looked at all the angels and gurgled happily.

*The Happy Family*

I introduced Robin and all the angels welcomed him warmly. They said they were delighted to have a new member of the team and that they were only too willing to help. Robin glowed with happiness and relief. He would prove to be a natural and stood by Freddie through many tough times.

Meanwhile, Winnie took some time to get over her difficult time in hospital. Bertie did what he could to help, although he was terrified of hurting the baby with his big strong hands. He soon got the hang of things and could be seen proudly pushing the pram round the village.

Right from the beginning, Winnie was determined to give Freddie the best start she possibly could. Money was always tight, so as well as doing his full time job, looking after their huge garden and an allotment, Bertie did a few gardening jobs in the village to earn a little extra cash. Winnie worked on the fruit farm part time and her mother cared for Freddie when needed.

Of course all the friends and relatives came to visit and in the days before the family had a telephone, they never knew who would turn up for Sunday lunch. Sometimes Pattie's mother and her new husband would come with their three children. Sometimes it would be Winnie's cousin Alice and her husband, Charles. Sometimes they all arrived together. The cry would go up: "Cut another cabbage, Bertie, and bring some more 'taters!"

On one such occasion, about eight people arrived. Winnie took all this in her stride and had luckily made two apple pies the previous day. However, making custard for twelve people is no mean feat. She made her custard in a huge mixing bowl and, when the time came, she plonked it on the table along with the pies. Alice was scandalised. Alice had no children and she and Charles were a bit 'posh' to her way of thinking. She, of course would have served the custard in a neat little jug. Alice tried to quietly complain that the mixing bowl was not really the thing, but our Winnie just about told her what she thought of that. Alice could then see that catering for twelve people did not allow for little jugs.

Freddie, meanwhile, was growing fast. The time had come for something to be done about her deformity. By the time she was eighteen months old, she had had two operations on her lip. Bertie couldn't bring himself to sign the consent form for the operations, as he said he didn't want to be responsible for not being able to recognise his little daughter.

Both operations were a success. The trouble had been that along with the cleft lip, because there was a hole in the roof of Freddie's mouth, feeding the baby had been very difficult as the milk would come down her nose. Once the cleft was closed, life became a great deal easier.

There was another problem to worry about. Many children with a cleft lip and palate have difficulty in speaking properly. The doctors told Winnie and Bertie that Freddie may need speech therapy.

When Freddie's grandfather heard about this, he said that no grandchild of his would have to go through that and he sat for hours with the little girl when she was old enough to talk, teaching her long complicated words like 'prehistoric monster' and 'Useless Eustace'. It seemed like a miracle that Freddie's speech did not seem to be affected at all. She was of course seen by the speech therapist at the big hospital, and on one occasion, the therapist showed the little girl some pictures and asked her to say what they were. Freddie, from the start, always had a vivid imagination and her own unique take on things, and so she got it into her head that the picture of a skirt that the therapist was showing her was actually a kilt and nothing would persuade her otherwise.

In fact her speech was thought to be so good for a child with a cleft lip and palate, that the therapist asked Winnie if she could record Freddie speaking so that she could take the recording on a lecture tour she was going to do in America. Robin was so proud.

In the early 1950s, there were some very clever plastic surgeons who had cared for fighter pilots who had been burnt during the War. One of these great men looked after Freddie's operations all during her childhood. When Freddie was four, she had the final operation to close the cleft in her lip. Robin, her angel, really came into his own when Freddie was in hospital.

He came to see Father God on one occasion, when Horace and I were making one of our reports. He excitedly told Father God how brave Freddie had been in hospital and how she had made friends with a slightly older boy who read the letters that Winnie wrote to her every day. What he didn't say was how he had been with Freddie all the time she was having her operation, lovingly sending her sweet dreams through the anaesthetic. He also tried to supervise the surgeon's Guardian Angel, to make sure nothing would go wrong. This, however did not go down too well with that angel, who turned out to be Jabez. Jabez told him that he knew what he was doing and perhaps it might be as well to concentrate on keeping Freddie safe and happy.

I knew this already as Jabez and I talked together sometimes. He had asked me who the young upstart was, and I explained how well Robin was doing, considering his shaky start. Jabez said that of course he forgave Robin and would look out for him if Freddie had to go into hospital again.

Winnie was fierce in the protection of her little daughter. She was visiting one sunny afternoon and all the children in the ward were playing outside on the lawn. All except Freddie, who was sitting sadly on her bed. Winnie sat on the bed beside her and, putting her arm round her, asked what the matter was. Freddie said that a kind lady had given her some soap, shaped like a cartoon dog. The problem was, as Freddie saw it, the soap was covered in coloured paint and she thought she had to scrape it off before she could use it. One of the nurses saw the mess that had been made and smacked Freddie hard. Winnie was furious. She went to the ward sister and made a terrible fuss. No one was going to hurt her daughter and they had better understand that!

Whenever he saw that particular nurse coming anywhere near Freddie, Robin would stand in front of his little charge with his wings spread, making the air around the bed electric, so the nurse felt uncomfortable and suddenly remembered she had something else to do.

Freddie had to go to the big hospital quite often in her early years. She was seen by the surgeon, who usually had several medical students with him. Freddie always remembered the sharp pencil that he used as a pointer to show the students the various areas on her face which had been operated upon. The surgeon was a very kindly man, and in her later life, Freddie remembered him with affection.

When she was about eight, she had to go to see an orthodontist. This was also a very clever man who had been asked to try to straighten her top teeth which were crooked due to the cleft palate. This meant that Winnie would take Freddie to the big town sometimes monthly. As I mentioned earlier, money was tight. Sarah knew this, and one day she said to Winnie that there was always a ten pound note in her coat pocket. It was there so that "that little girl" could get to the hospital. Winnie never took it, but she loved her Aunt Sarah even more for her kindness.

During the long bus trips to hospital, Winnie would make up little games to help pass the time. They would count the cows in the fields, or play 'I Spy'. Winnie would have a few mints in her pocket and they would have a competition to see who could make their mint last longest.

After the appointment with the orthodontist, they would go into the big restaurant in the High Street, and have tomato soup and a bread roll for lunch. It was only in her later years that Freddie realised that this was all her mother could afford. As a young child, apart from the unpleasantness of the various appointments, Freddie always regarded these trips to the big town as a sort of adventure. This was in no small part due to Winnie's genius at making the whole thing an occasion.

This was a valuable life lesson: to be satisfied with the small things and to make a little go a long way. Freddie also learned the art of hospitality from her mother. Winnie's door was open to anyone in need and there seemed to be a great variety of strange people banging on the back door.

# Chapter 5

# Winnie's Strange Visitors

As the family lived in the country, quite a few of the things they needed were delivered.

One of Freddie's favourites was the baker who came twice a week with fresh bread. Their dog liked him too, because the baker would very often bring him a stale doughnut. They never knew the man's name, always just calling him 'baker'.

On Saturday mornings, Don would come. This was a man who delivered paraffin in the days when most people had paraffin heaters (very handy in the outside loo). He also had a van which was like an Aladdin's cave. He sold polish and dusters, soap powder, a few tools and all manner of useful bits and pieces. If Winnie needed something she thought Don might have on his van, she would take Freddie to have a look. Freddie thought this was marvellous. She loved to explore in the van and look at all the wonderful things.

Of course now we would just pop to the supermarket for whatever we need, but then it was a real service that people like Don provided.

Then there was Mr. Hall who was the 'insurance man'. He must have been super fit, as he cycled everywhere on a very smart racing bike with drop handlebars. Freddie was fascinated by the yellow cycling cape he wore when it was raining.

Every month or so, the coal man would arrive, carrying a hundredweight of coal on his back. This was a sack of coal that weighed 112 pounds. His partner would ease the sack from the lorry onto a leather saddle on the coal man's shoulders. Everyone in the village had an open fire, so this was another great service. The coal man would carry the sack to an outside coal bunker and tip it in with a thunderous crash. It was Bertie's job to fill up the coal scuttle which stood by the fire.

One winter, it started snowing on Boxing Day and didn't really stop until Easter. Everyone found it really difficult to get around as the roads were icy and the snow drifted deeply every night. I had a word with the Angels in the Weather Regulation Department, but they said they couldn't do much about it because there was a new Angel in the Snowflake Development Office and he had got a bit carried away. Father God had already spoken to him about it, but by this time everyone was knee deep in snow.

It was on one of these arctic days that the coal man and his young helper were trying to do their round. They had found it harder than ever to get to the village and, when they arrived at Winnie's door, they were both exhausted. Winnie asked them in to have a cup of tea and to get warm. The coal man said, "No, Missus, thank you kindly, but we're late as it is and we've got to get this coal delivered before it gets dark."

Winnie glared at him fiercely. "Are you trying to kill this youngster?" she said. "Look at him, he can hardly stand up. Get in here, the pair of you and have a rest, for Goodness' sake!"

I was very quickly realising that when Winnie was in one of her fierce moods, you just didn't argue. The two tired men came in and gratefully sat by the fire, while Winnie made them steaming cups of tea with plenty of sugar and a huge cheese sandwich. They stayed for about half-an-hour and then felt much more able to carry on with their heavy work.

This was typical of Winnie. She was the soul of generosity and there were many people in the village who were thankful for her kindness.

So it was for a 'gentleman of the road' (or tramp) called Paddy. He was well known in the area and so knew where he could usually get something to eat. Whenever

Paddy came to Winnie's back door, he was always assured of a hot drink and a sandwich. "Thank'ee indeed Ma'am," he would say, and continue on his way.

There was a man in the village whose name was Bert, but was known as Daisy for some reason. Daisy had been left to fend for himself since he was a boy and the villagers did their best to look out for him. If anyone had an old coat or some unwanted jumpers, Daisy was always grateful to receive them. He was another occasional visitor to Winnie's door. Sometimes he would bring a cabbage or some eggs as a gift, although it was not always clear where the things had come from. Quite often there was a gap in someone's allotment, or eggs mysteriously disappeared from underneath a person's chickens. Everybody knew who had taken them, but nobody seemed to mind.

Bertie knew Daisy well, as he had been called up into the same Regiment during the war. The trouble was that Daisy kept escaping or going AWOL (absent without leave), as he couldn't bear to be cooped up in the barracks. He had lived rough most of his life and having a roof over his head was just too much. On more than one occasion, Bertie had been told to go and bring him back, but of course by then he was filthy. It was then Bertie's job to clean him up. Daisy would regale anyone who would listen with stories of how Bertie had hosed him down and didn't seem at all embarrassed.

As Winnie's Guardian Angel, I became more and more proud of her. On my visits to Father God, I would tell Him of her acts of kindness and He would tell St. Peter to record them in his book. God loved her very much, as He loves all of His children, and He looked forward to hearing about her latest good deed.

There were several other visitors who left feeling better than when they arrived. One of these was an Indian gentleman called Shen Singh. He had served in the British

Army during the war, but now was unable to return home. He lived in a very old caravan in the next village and earned a meagre living by cycling round the district with a huge suitcase on the front of his bike containing ladies' cardigans, stockings and underwear, which he would sell door-to-door. Whenever he came to Winnie's house, she of course invited him in, and out would come the teapot. She seemed to know that Shen was very lonely and what he needed more than anything was a bit of human contact. She would chat to him while he was drinking his tea, and he would tell her about India and his life there before the war.

He always wore an army greatcoat and Freddie would sit next to him, listening to his stories. On one of his visits, he brought Freddie some seeds. He said he didn't know if they would grow in Britain, but they were pretty flowers which were very common in his native land. Bertie had a go at growing them but they obviously didn't like the British climate.

Then there was Mrs. Cooper and her daughter. These ladies were gypsies who made and sold wooden clothes pegs and sprays of dried lavender. Every couple of years or so, the Gypsies would stop in their travels and come into the village. Winnie liked to see them, and naturally, tea was the order of the day.

This was another valuable lesson for Freddie. Her mother never judged anyone and she made everyone welcome, no matter where they came from or what their background. It was also interesting for Horace and I to meet angels from another culture. Neither Shen nor Mrs. Cooper knew about Jesus, but Father God gave them Guardians anyway, the same as He did for all of His children. This was further proof, as if it were needed, of Father God's total love for everyone.

I think here is a good place to tell you about Uncle Joe. Joe was an old bachelor who lived in the house next door. His mother had lived in the house for many years and in her old age was not able to care for herself. Even when Winnie was pregnant she used to go and do what she could for the old lady. Unfortunately the house was filthy and, when Winnie went into hospital to have her baby, she had flea bites all over her legs.

When Joe's mother died, Winnie and Bertie continued to look out for him. He would come in on weekend mornings for his cup of tea. The dog, Pippy, liked Joe too, and also enjoyed his tea. He had his own little enamel dish and liked to see a spoonful of sugar put in. What he really liked, however, was for Joe to stir the tea with his finger. Now Joe was an old country man and his hands were never very clean. This didn't bother Pip at all. Perhaps it enhanced the flavour.

Joe had a very deep country accent. He was also full of country sayings. For instance he would describe a very dark night as, "black as the devil's nutting bag." Dark clouds were, "black over our Will's mother's." He also liked his beer. Sometimes he could be heard singing loudly through the connecting wall.

One weekend, Winnie and Bertie had been decorating their living room. Joe came in quite late in the evening to see how they were getting on. It was quite obvious that he had just come home from the pub. He stood in the middle of the room, turning round and round, looking at the new green paint on the doors and picture rail. "Ooh I say, Win," he said. "That's nice, innit? Will it be the same pattern as the wallpaper when it dries?" "You daft old thing!" she laughed. "Go home and sleep it off and come back in the morning!"

The reason he was known as Uncle Joe, was that he was Freddie's godfather. Winnie had a vague idea that this might bring him closer to God, as at some point in his life he had been a church-goer. It didn't seem to work, though. However, he was always kind to Freddie and remembered her at Christmas and her birthday. Joe's angel was called Algernon and he taught all of us angels about country life. By this time, there was a whole crowd of Guardian Angels caring for the family and their friends. It was marvellous to be able to support each other.

There were Dick and Harry, Winnie's parents' angels; Horace and me, Robin, Freddie's angel and Algernon, who might as well have lived in Winnie's house, as Joe was there so often. Then there were all the angels assigned to the visitors. Cedric and Wilberforce came with Pattie and John and there were whole tribes of others when everyone came for Sunday lunch. We all knew that Father God was looking over us all in His kindly way and we were happy.

Winnie, Bertie and Joe liked to play cards in the evening. They especially enjoyed it when

*Freddie and Pattie*

Pattie and her husband John came to stay for the weekend. Winnie was a very good card player and Horace and I watched, fascinated, as the cards were dealt and the game progressed. The only problem with this was that she was a lot sharper mentally than Joe and everyone had to keep a good eye on her so that she didn't cheat. This was all done in the spirit of fun, though, and their roars of laughter could be heard at the bottom of the garden. If Winnie had been caught cheating, Joe would wipe the tears of laughter from his eyes, and say, "Do that again, Gel, and I'll catch thee a whack a'thert the 'ed with a sy-ringe!" No one had a clue what he was talking about, but it set everyone off into new gales of merriment.

And so, life went on. Freddie went to the village school and was very happy there. It seemed that not much had changed in the school since Winnie was a pupil. This was a real problem, as more and more children were coming to the village and the old school was becoming more and more dilapidated. Before long, the childrens' classes were spread between the old school, a converted stable at the back of the priest's house, and a huge room in the Big House.

The Big House was home to the squire. The family were descended from a real saint, and they were proper aristocrats. The squire's mother and her sister were wonderfully generous to the poorer village people and there was many a family who were helped through tough times with a food parcel or warm blankets.

Winnie's mother was briefly a house maid in the Big House many years before and, on one occasion, Miss Mary, the squire's aunt, came to visit her when she was ill. Bertie always stood up when she came in and touched his forelock. Now this is a very old fashioned sign of respect. Winnie respected the family too, but when Miss Mary was leaving and said to Freddie, "Open the door for me, dear," Winnie said firmly, "I'll teach my daughter her manners, Miss Mary, if you don't mind."

I must say that Horace and I laughed so much we couldn't speak. This was so typical of our dear Winnie.

# Chapter 6

# St. Thomas and the Currant Buns

It was at this time that we had an amazing blessing from Father God. One day soon after this, God sent for Horace, Robin and me. When we arrived at God's beautiful room there, standing before the Throne, was a most dignified person. "Ah, here you are," said Our Father. "I want to introduce you to my dear friend Thomas. The family in the Big House in your village know him as Saint Thomas More. They are direct descendants. I made him a Saint many hundreds of years ago and he is very well known all over the world. I have asked him to tell you about some of the history of the village and some of his adventures with King Henry the Eighth."

We were astonished. The dignified gentleman turned to us and grinned. "Hello, young angels," he said. "We'll have some good talk together. Come with me."

We all bowed to our Father and Saint Thomas led us to the big oak tree we knew so well. We all sat in the shade and Thomas began to talk. He told us about the sheep and wool trade in the Middle Ages, which was the way the people earned their living in the village for hundreds of years. He told about the path along the Downs, which had been a main trade route for people on foot, or with pack animals for thousands of years. He explained how the general area had been loyal to the King during the Civil War. He also told us that there was a secret in the Big House.

He said there was a time when it was against the law to be a Catholic in the country. More than that, if a priest was caught, he would be put to death. The family in the Big House had a chapel where Mass was said all during the troubled times. The Chapel was cleverly disguised as a woodshed and was never discovered. There was also what was known as a 'priest hole'. This was a tiny space hidden in a wall or under floor boards, where a priest could be safely hidden.

We were fascinated. It was wonderful to learn more about where our people lived and it was amazing to hear all this history from a great Saint. I shyly asked how Saint Thomas came to Heaven. He told us, "Well, King Henry was a very strong character. I had served in his Government for many years. He wanted more than anything an heir to the throne but his wife was not able to produce a male baby, so he wanted to divorce her. He asked the Pope to dissolve the marriage, but of course, the Pope refused. This was the beginning of all the religious troubles. King Henry made himself leader of the church and many people were executed for disagreeing with him. I was one of them. I was a prisoner in the Great Tower for several years and, in the end, they cut off my head. It is just as well that we are all made perfect again when we get to Heaven, don't you think?"

Saint Thomas roared with laughter at his own joke and we couldn't help laughing with him.

Thomas then said, "If you are quick, you will be able to see a custom which goes back hundreds of years. Today is Shrove Tuesday. This is the day that people would eat up anything they had which they were not allowed to eat during Lent. Go now. Freddie will be taking part." With that, Saint Thomas More got up, gave us a cheery wave and walked off through the wood, humming to himself.

Horace watched Thomas go. "There goes a very happy man," he said, smiling affectionately. "Come on," I said. "Let's go and see what Saint Thomas was talking about. Besides, I don't like leaving Winnie too long. You never know what she'll get up to next."

We took Robin by the hands and flew back to the village. We knew that the children were in school, so we went to find out what was going on.

Outside the old school building, there were several dozen mothers and fathers waiting to see what would happen. We joined the great cluster of Guardians, fluttering around excitedly. All at once we heard many children chattering and laughing as they poured out of the school gate. They lined up, two-by-two, and set off singing down the hill from the school.

The little rhyme that they sang was hundreds of years old and went like this:

> *Pit pat the pancake.*
> *Here we go a'shroving.*
> *With the butcher up me back*
> *A ha'penny's better than nothing.*

All the angels followed, wondering where the children were going. We soon realised that they were going to the Big House. They walked up the drive, still singing their song. Outside the main door, the squire and his mother stood behind a long table which was loaded with dozens of currant buns. They smiled as they gave each child a bun and then a coin. This was called a halfpenny piece or a ha'penny.

This custom had been happening in the village as long as anyone could remember. This, it seemed, was why Saint Thomas knew about it and wanted us to see it. You can probably guess that the village shop was swamped with children wanting to spend their ha'pennies on their way home.

Saint Thomas had also told us about the old chapel. It had been built many hundreds of years ago and there was a legend that there was a tunnel leading from there to the Big House. No one had ever found it but, as he said, legends have to start somewhere.

Freddie passed the chapel everyday on her way home from school. Next to it a war memorial had been built to honour all the young men who had lost their lives in both wars. Each year on Remembrance Sunday a wreath of poppies was laid on the memorial. One year Bertie was proud to be asked to lay the wreath. Horace was proud too, standing as close to Bertie as he could to give him encouragement as he was very nervous. Bertie marched down the village to the memorial and, when the time came, laid the wreath with military precision. Winnie felt quite emotional as her brother was mentioned there. Each year she would place a small wooden cross decorated with a poppy with her brother's name and naval number written on it. She also made sure that Pattie knew from a very young age that her father's name was recorded on the memorial.

Winnie's little family always enjoyed joining in with events in the village. There was the yearly village feast when a small fair set up in the field next to the public house. This was a very modest affair, but the children thought it was marvellous.

Freddie's favourite though, was the Donkey Derby. In a field next to the Big House, a course was laid out and donkeys from all over the district came for the occasion. They were given funny names, and the races were treated as if the donkeys were race horses.

Lads from the racing stables were the riders and if they could get the donkeys to move at all, there were prizes for the winners. Most of the village people looked forward to the Donkey Derby and there was usually a good crowd to cheer the donkeys on.

There was a summer party in the gardens of the Big House, and the children had a wonderful time, coming home tired out and covered in grass stains from rolling down the bank.

Freddie's memories of her childhood were always tinged with a great love for her father. Bertie was a man of very few words, but he loved his daughter dearly. When Freddie was quite little, Bertie fitted a saddle to the cross bar on his bike and Freddie remembered riding with him all over the place. He would take her to the Sunday afternoon cricket matches and let her help him keep the scores. He took her for walks, just the two of them, as he had done for Pattie all those years ago.

*Freddie and her Daddy on holiday*

Everyone still loved to go and see Aunt Sarah. If anyone had a birthday, or at Christmas, their first thought was to take their cards to show Sarah and Emily. Emily was, by this time, even more dependent. She was unable to feed herself and deafer than ever. She still sat by the fire and would love to put Winnie's gloves on and hold Pip the dog's lead. Freddie was quite often called upon to sing. Nursery rhymes, little songs she had learned at school, it didn't matter. Sarah so enjoyed hearing the songs and thought they were wonderful, just because it was Freddie singing them.

And so Freddie grew up surrounded with love and security. Winnie remembered how tough her own childhood had been and saw to it that Freddie was given the childhood that she never had.

Freddie had a special friend called Ronnie. She and her angel Roland very often came for Sunday tea. During the school holidays, Ronnie virtually lived at the house. She and

Freddie played together contentedly, living in their own imaginary world.

While life was good for Freddie, this was not so for her mother. Winnie found that her own mother was becoming less and less able to take care of herself, and naturally, the burden of care fell at Winnie's feet.

# Chapter 7

# Winnie Goes Home

Winnie's mother had always been a difficult person to live with. As she got older, her mind began to fail. One of the problems was that she was very deaf. She had a hearing aid, but very often refused to wear it. Communicating with her became harder and harder. As she couldn't hear what was being said, she assumed that people were talking about her and this caused a great deal of unpleasantness.

The other problem was that she depended on Winnie for everything, but still thought that she was in charge of the household. This made the situation at home almost impossible sometimes. Winnie naturally became very frustrated and if it wasn't for Bertie's steady and kind influence, she wouldn't have been able to cope at all.

This went on for years. Towards the end of her mother's life, the old lady was bed-ridden. There was still no outside help to be had and so Winnie was totally responsible for her care, night and day. Winnie's father had died some years before and she had looked after him as well. It seemed to her that her life was completely taken up with care for other people.

There were some lighter moments, however. Like the time that Winnie nearly got arrested!

There was a coach outing to the seaside one year. Winnie and several other ladies decided to go together. When they arrived, they all bought 'kiss-me-quick' hats with feathers in them and a fair bit of alcohol was consumed. They were having such a good time that their picture was taken and appeared in the next evening's newspaper. There they were, strolling along the promenade, when who should wander along beside them but a policeman. Winnie and her friends fell into step behind him, copying the way he walked. Fortunately, he turned out to be a friendly policeman and laughed when he realised what they were doing.

While we are on the subject of coach outings, one summer evening there was what was called a 'Mystery Tour'. In those days, as very few people had cars, coach trips were very popular. Winnie and Freddie got tickets to go and so did Winnie's mother as she was still able at the time.

After a lovely ride, on the way back a huge electrical thunderstorm hit. The lightening was spectacular, but also very scary, as the forked lightening appeared to strike to ground all around the coach and sheet lightening surrounded it with a bright flash of what looked like thick fog. Everyone had got home safely, when suddenly Bertie came in, dripping wet. He had been on the night shift at the little railway station, and had cycled home through the worst of the storm to make sure everyone was safe. Horace, Robin and I looked at each other in amazement. We could hardly believe that we had seen such love. You may depend that Father God heard about this as soon as we could get to Him.

I also explained to our Father in Heaven that Winnie was becoming exhausted and depression was threatening again. She had a part-time job cleaning the new school by this time, was looking after her mother, going to help put Emily to bed and she still found time for another kindness.

I told Father God that she had been to the next village where Percy's family lived. They had four children, but not much idea of how to look after them. Not only that, housekeeping was not their mother's strong point and they lived in squalor. Squalor is when living conditions become filthy and there is no comfort in a home.

On more than one occasion, Winnie had got on her bike with a box on the back filled with cleaning cloths, bleach, polish and anything she could think of for the task of cleaning the family's home up.

Father God was filled with love for Winnie. He asked me to take some of my Heavenly friends to guard her at night and help to strengthen her by day. He also told me to whisper in her ear about going to the doctor to tell him how she felt. I bowed to my Father and went to do as He told me.

Winnie did eventually see the doctor and after a course of tablets began to feel better and more able to cope with her busy life.

Meanwhile, the family had had some good news. Freddie had passed the eleven-plus which was an exam eleven-year-old children took to see which school they would go to after primary school. Winnie and Bertie really wanted Freddie to be able to go to the convent grammar school. If she passed the eleven-plus she would be able to have a grant. If she didn't, she would either have to go to the secondary modern school or they would have to pay for her to go to the convent. They would have paid somehow, but it would have crippled them. You can imagine the family's joy when they got the news.

Freddie attended the convent school and was happy there. Ronnie remained her best friend all the time. They listened to music together, went for walks and generally enjoyed each other's company. Ronnie was two classes above Freddie at the convent, being that much older. They remain friends to this day.

At seventeen, Freddie left school and after a while she left home to start training as a nurse and this is where we say goodbye to her. It was a very difficult time for Winnie and Bertie. Depression was never far away at this point in Winnie's life and she missed Freddie dreadfully.

We angels missed Robin, too. He had developed so well from the nervous little scrap that he had been when we first met him. He was now confident and strong and he told us that he would do his best to look after Freddie in her new life. We knew he would and we all went to see Father God as we said goodbye to him.

No matter how Winnie felt, she still had her mother to care for. Emily died, closely followed by Sarah. This was a great sadness for Winnie, as Sarah had been a great support for her for most of her life. Freddie visited as often as she could, but it wasn't the same as having her at home. What Winnie missed most was the way Freddie made her laugh. Freddie had always been the family clown and Winnie would laugh until she cried at her antics.

Then came the time that Winnie's mother died. Winnie said that all she could feel was relief. Of course she was sad that her mother was dead, but she had given so much to her care that she was totally worn out. It took her several months to feel anything like herself again, but then she and Bertie took themselves off for a proper seaside holiday, the first they had had since Freddie was a little girl.

They began to enjoy village life again. They sometimes went to a club with some friends and once they went to an evening of old time music, where everyone dressed up. Bertie went so far as to wear a bow tie.

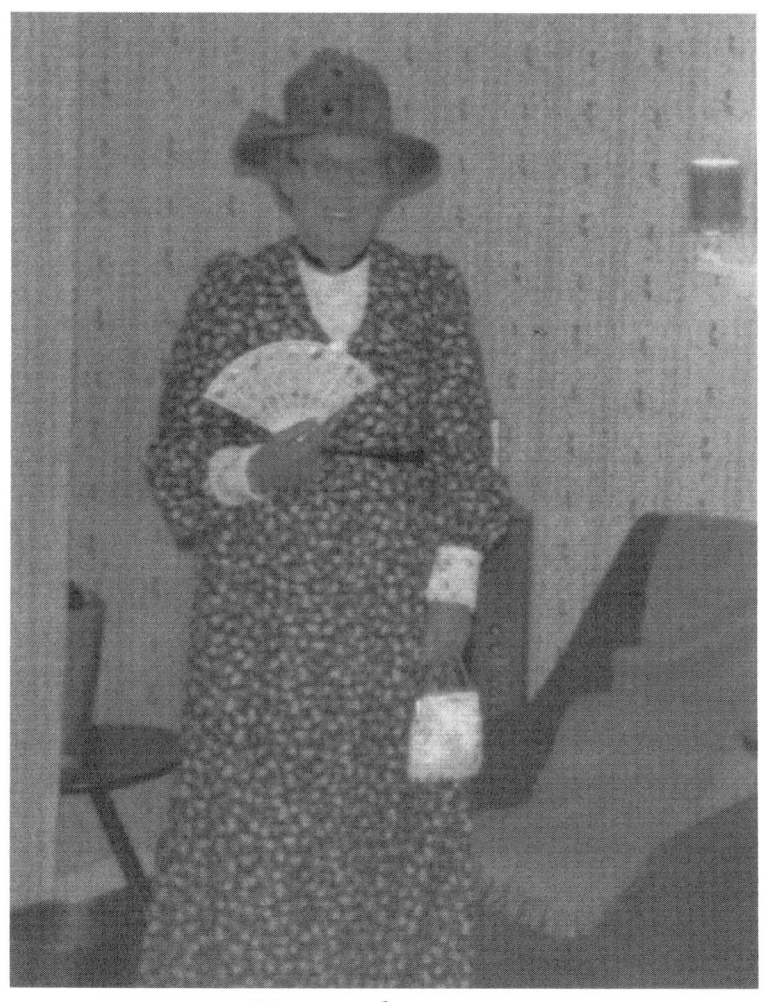

*Winnie dresses up*

They both decided that they would like to learn how to make wine. Bertie bought a book and they collected the equipment they would need. They made wine alright. The friends who tried it said it was lethal!

They learned how to preserve their vegetables for freezing and Winnie made some lovely marmalade. They were still busy, but they were happy.

Winnie also went to sewing classes. Bertie bought her an electric sewing machine and she made dresses and skirts for herself and Freddie. This was a time when capes were the fashion and Winnie made Freddie a very smart black and white cape, lined with shiny red, with a skirt to match.

Pattie and John were fairly frequent visitors and by this time they had two children. Bertie loved to take John to the pub on a Sunday lunchtime and show him off to the locals. It meant a great deal to him that this young man would pay him this attention.

He was very fond of John and talked to him almost more than to anyone else.

Now comes a very sad part in our story. Winnie and Bertie were happy together for about five years. One day, Horace said to me, "I don't think Bertie is very well, you know." He wasn't. Poor Bertie had a heart attack that day, and although he recovered from it, he was never the same again. He slowly got worse over the next couple of years, and died in the hospital in the big town.

This was the last straw for Winnie. She had had a big operation during the same year and was not in good health herself. Bertie had been her rock all their married life. She loved him dearly and now he was gone. Freddie was married by now and she and her husband did what they could to support her and so did Pattie and John, but the light had gone out of her and all she wanted was to be with her Bertie.

She got that wish on the day that I carried her soul to Heaven, when she had died after a long illness.

It had been a privilege to be her Guardian Angel for so many years. She had taught me so much about human kindness and there were many people who genuinely mourned her passing. She was missed by the whole village. Friends and relatives came from all over the country to her funeral, and Robin, Horace, Wilberforce, Cedric, Tom, Dick and Harry and all the other Angels who had known and loved her joined in the service and helped sing her soul to Paradise.

This book was produced by

# WORDS by DESIGN

www.wordsbydesign.co.uk

Words by Design offers a range of services to individual and corporate clients, as well as to the printing and publishing industry.

In a digital age, authors wish to publish their own books; families seek to research and write the history of their ancestors; businesses see the marketing significance of commissioning their corporate history; and publishers use freelance experts in all the many varied stages of publishing.

At Words by Design we have the necessary experience and knowledge to help with these and many other projects. With expertise in research, writing, editing, design, photography, typesetting and print production, we aim to be able to help on any project.

office@wordsbydesign.co.uk
+44 (0)1869 327548